Your Brain Cells Sing
When They Die

Carina Hart

Your Brain Cells Sing When They Die

THE **BLACK SPRING**
PRESS GROUP

First published in 2021
by the Black Spring Press Group
Grantully Road, Maida Vale, London W9,
United Kingdom

This imprint: Eyewear Poetry

Typeset with graphic design by Edwin Smet
Author photograph Claire Lloyd

ISBN 978-1-913606-90-9

BLACKSPRINGPRESSGROUP.COM

Part III: At the Level of Desire

YOUR BRAIN CELLS SING WHEN THEY DIE

What price a supernova?
Just take a drink of aspartame
to fire up those neurotransmitters,
two hundred times sweeter than sugar.

Just for a drink of aspartame,
your brain cells sing when they die.
Two hundred times sweeter than sugar
with excitotoxins to finish you off.

Your brain cells sing when they die,
as caffeine and aspartame collide;
the excitotoxins finish you off
with a fizzing, irresistible song.

When caffeine and aspartame collide
they are, as you know, the bomb.
Exploding in a fizzing, irresistible song —
your brain cells sing when they die.

And the known unknown of the bomb
is what keeps you coming back:
your brain cells sing when they die,
and we all know the words to the song.

So it keeps you coming back
because it's already half forgotten —
we all knew the words to the song,
but now we're not so sure.

Because it's already half forgotten,
though your brain cells sang as they died.
A cosmic experience, to be sure,
but what price a supernova?

Part I
Sanctioned Solace

AGENDA

- Item 1: to decide if we can take this forward.

- Apologies: I can't accept your apologies, when every day your absence makes things harder to discuss.

- I apologise for tabling this again – actually, no apologies: I'm tired of being the one who pushes forward, through all the things you refuse to discuss.

- Like that awful birthday, when we agreed – both of us – that I shouldn't have to ask for attention, and then you didn't even meet me at the station. You didn't even meet me on that freezing night, after we'd agreed.

- No, I don't want your apologies, when the point was I shouldn't have to ask for them.

- I don't think I want to meet again. There's nothing to agree.

- Just one thing though, so I can move forward: aren't you sorry that it all went –

- aren't you sorry there was nothing we could agree, in the end; that nothing in us could meet?

MINUTES

- It was confirmed as the last time we would meet. All parties ultimately agreed there were no further items to discuss.

- There were no apologies.

- There was a discussion point on apologies, unresolved. Only one party was able to table questions, so talks could not move forward.

- But it was silly to talk of moving forwards. You only looked backwards – that awful birthday again, demanding apologies so that I can't give them, really. I can't meet you in the freezing night; if you demand agreement then I haven't agreed.

- There was nothing for me in what you wanted, so I won't apologise for not meeting your needs.

- Looking forward, I saw a life strung out on apologies once the process was begun.

- I can't agree to be sorry there was nothing we could discuss. I'm only sorry for all the apologies –

- given and not given, sorry that apologies were all there was. I don't know why we couldn't just agree, in the end, that nothing in us could meet.

PRESENTATION

You have fifteen seconds to make your impression,
research has shown. Check your teeth for signs of
carelessness; apply the precise nuance
of lipstick to convey professionalism,
and a touch more to show willing.
Pull down the rucked skirt – propriety is best –
and pull down the shirt for the requisite
level of sex. It's the finest balance:
heels should be three inches high, research has shown.
Check you can walk. Your attention to
detail can be seen in your mascara:
no clumps there; smooth down that curl of hair
that might betray an insubordination.
Check your face again for imperfection.
Ready. What were you were going to say?

HOW TO SERVICE A COMMITTEE

I.   Hierarchy is key. You must begin
      at the top, and learn the particular
      preferences of this committee; but
      you must be equally attentive to
      all members as you work your way
      down.

II.   The Chair is where it all begins and ends:
      all powers ultimately rest here.
      You must keep the Committee Chair
      in hand, but be sure to remember
      that they remain above you
      at all times.

III. It is your responsibility
      to ensure that all required actions
      are fulfilled by the designated
      member. Do not assume that the agenda
      will take care of itself without your
      assistance.

IV.   It is particularly crucial that all
      matters arising are worked towards a
      conclusion on time. We are, after all,
      under tight constraints. And please bear in mind
      that someone will want to use the room
      after you.

CONCRETE POEM

actually I
might just
delete it
all yes

I've still
got six
minutes to
sit here

it'll do
you really
can't straighten
up again

god why
don't they
just straighten
up again

her little
face all
lit up
and then

one hundred
and thirty-
four days
to go

all the
single ladies
all the
single ladies

she won't
feel the
effects just
yet but

if he
does it
today I
will just

it's because
these other
idiots can't
park straight

it might
be wrong
they might
not see

I can't
I can't
I can't
I can't

under the
tree but
I'll be
first out

oh look
at the
birds in
the sun

do they
drink tea
with milk
in Brno

no one
will see
me eat
lunch here

20:20

twenty minutes
twenty metres
twenty seconds
that is the measure
of my sanctioned solace
every twenty minutes
I can look up and out
from my inbox scrolldown
flags and figures
and swap my outlook for the sun
where it dances
on twenty metres of grass
waving at me
beholden to none
and touching the houses with light
so that they are my horizon
and I'm tricked into thinking
that's where freedom starts but
at least for twenty seconds I can see
that clearly

SOLACE

I worked late
this Bonfire Night,
alone and staring in
the dark as hot points of
anger multiplied on screen.
But walking home I had to stop
and turn to watch the fireworks I
thought I'd missed. Fifteen minutes
standing in the middle of the street, caught
in light as golden arms reached long and bright
and grew fingers out towards me. Hands and knees
froze solid but my eyes were full of fire, learning a lesson
in how moments work – they multiply, then gone. But on and on
and still I stood, in the solace of total refraction,
while person after person, faces dark
in silhouette, walked
the other way.

NIGHT PEOPLE

From an idea by Jean Shepherd

Night people
don't want to be night people,
usually; they are the sitting dead,
desperate at their desks while the daylight ebbs away.

They are medicated, usually;
agreements swallowed
with cold coffee, cells deleted
with painkiller formulae,
internet tranquilisers
shutting down neurons, firing blank after blank after

this is over they can live,
eking out the night: minutes
rolled slowly over the tongue
where luxury tastes of peach;
slow-roasted thoughts
and sudden sherbet laughter fizzing in the nose, finally
awake.

But when life is this short, dissolved
in tiny parma violets
in the smallest hours,
the tip of the tongue is not enough
and night people, eventually, will seek the endless feast.

DEFINITIONS

1. The ruler measures my desk.
2. The ruler defines the limits of my space.
3. The ruler decides the meaning of all space.
4. The ruler is an authority in these matters.
5. The ruler is an authority on all matter.
6. The ruler is the author of all things.
7. The ruler applies its rule to all things.
8. The rule of the ruler applies to itself.
9. The ruler creeps millimetre by millimetre to the edge of its known universe.
10. Thirty centimetres.

GOOD ADMINISTRATION

Good administration has no smell.
No one eats houmous at this desk;
we do not cultivate flowers
or atmospheres.

Good administration has no taste.
Everyone is too busy to eat and
more abstract kinds of taste are
not required either.

Good administration does not touch.
It will not touch you, it is
not touched or touching; it is
untouchable.

Good administration has no sound.
Not even the rustle of a memo.
We are paperless now.

Good administration is not seen.
Things just work.

Until they don't,
and the message doesn't get through
before the contractors leave,
and the whole thing goes up in flames,
and the stench is that of administration,
bitter charcoal coating tongues and
flakes of red tape between fingers;
everyone's heard how bad the admin is
and now we see its black heart;

but every administrator knows
they did their part.

CHANGE MANAGEMENT WITH NOAH

And the Lord said
there must be a top-down rationalisation
by way of fully managed precipitation;
sweep away, root and branch, the old ways.

And the Lord said
processes have been mapped and found inadequate:
the organisation cannot thus move forward.
Below management level all structures must go.

And the Lord said
let it rain for forty days and forty nights
precisely; my executive schedule is tight.
I will wipe from the earth every living creature I have
made.

And the Lord said
the redundancies are most regrettable,
but every bird and beast must be accountable
in the final audit.

And the Lord said
we have been much lauded for our transformation.
No there are no plans for reconstruction
until we secure funding for the next phase.

TAKING THE BLAME

I stole your pen. It was gathering queries.
I stole your eraser. It was gathering regrets.
I stole your hole-punch. It was gathering months of tiny moons,
        paper-white nights unused.
I stole your milk. It was going off.

I stole your mug. It was gathering moments of possible peace.
I stole your notepad. It was pale and blank and desperate.
I stole the one idea on it.
I stole your paperclips. I stole your bulldog clips. I stole your safety pins.
        I was falling apart
and I didn't want to take your valuable time.

PROCESS MAPPING

Identification of issues:

Failures of information management, due to a
>> leaky pipeline
>>> of neurons misfiring losing cognitive data;
memory files slowing systems when
>> clogged
>>> arteries slow oxygen flow to brain;
too many handoffs breaking
>> comms channels
>>> through inferior frontal gyrus –

Proposed solutions:

Process management must be fully
>> embedded
>>> recoding of cognitive associations;
rationalisation of production lines to
>> reduce waste
>>> products released into the bloodstream,
and strengthen existing network
>> connections
>>> linking neural pathways.

Implementation:

Process monitoring built in at every
                    approved stage
                                     of mindfulness training programme;
concentrate decision-making in top-down
                    chain of command
                                     controlling the prefrontal cortex;
most of these are surplus personnel –
                    in fact
                                     strip it all out and start again

SUNSET (VERB)

We are sunsetting this project.
We know it glowed, briefly, like
a cluster of wild roses in
the morning light; the way they sprout
sudden in untended ground,
ideas woken from soil sleep.

We know you tended its unfurling
with careful joy, planted firmly
in a timely pitch, presented
in the right light. The birds
started singing, here in the city;
you were bathed in sun, surprised.

But it's natural selection, you know,
dog eat dog world and the stakeholders
have pulled out, roots and all –
a new growth area has come
to light and you are eclipsed.
It's not all roses in this life,

you know, and the bottom line,
the bottom line is always in the shade.
We are sunsetting this project.
If you look out of the window
now, you might still catch
the last of the light.

TO THE CLOUD

the cloud

back it up to   so we can move

    consolidate this   forward

      blue sky   thinking

           into transparent policy

   bedded down   saved

          at the coalface   give it a dry run

    in the sandbox

   realise it   into concrete process

as a legacy development

                it's your baby

        bed it in   push on this

   to realise it

online-only   forever

    will be in the cloud

         blue sky

   move forward   thinking

          as transparent

    legacy development policy

gave it a dry run

      bedded down

        online-only

consolidate this   saved

    at the coalface

   to realise   in the sandbox

    it's your baby

push on this   process

    into concrete

   bed it in

   realise it   will be in the cloud

             forever

PERFORMANCE REVIEW

I have come to expect settings here to be commendably minimalist. This time the curtain rose on a surprising quantity of paper for this day and age, and an ill-advised orchid.

It began with targets – the performer wavered. The targets were esoteric and anyone would have struggled with that script.

The dialogue on time allocation was implausible: who spends six hours a week writing minutes? That would be forty-one working days per year. One year and four months over a forty-year career, solid minutes.

At this point I had to slip out for a gin and tonic.

The challenges scene is always awkward. The performer verged on shrill in pushing how challenging the challenges were: they could not quite row back to convince us they could meet them.

The performer seemed strained.

There was insufficient build-up to the climax: *And are you happy?* Bold choice for the final question.

There was a pause too long and the whole performance faltered.

EVERYTHING IS SLIPPING AWAY FROM ME

YOU'RE IN CONTROL

SIGN UP TODAY

Create an automatic backup strategy
that fits your schedule and requirements
with our cutting-edge software!

Back up all the files on your system
with one of several systematic options,
and never lose your most important files!

SIGN UP TODAY

YOU'RE IN CONTROL

BOXES OF LIGHT*

I am the last pair of eyes
to assess your application
before I consign it
to the process.
Now you have encoded
yourself in our form
[folded flesh into boxes]
I can open you up
and recode you in light:
in this form
you can go anywhere.

I am the last pair of eyes
who will read you,
though you will continue
to be read.

Mine are the last corneas
through which you will pass
like sun in a window, through
the last strata of membranes
[epithelium
Bowman's
stroma
Descemet's
endothelium]
the last funhouse mirrors
in which you are reflected,
tiny and upside down like
a foetus, waiting.

Mine are the last irises
to draw wide like curtains
in the morning; the last

pupils to usher you in.
Mine are the last retinas
to refract you into
a million separate light impulses
to travel through
a million nerve endings
along a million nerve fibres
to be gathered in my optic nerve.
There I can put you back together
and make sense of you.
When I have seen you
I will make my decision.

I am the last pair of eyes, so
you may be sure I will look carefully.

When I have seen you
I press a key and turn you
into something else. I enter you
into the box of boxes,
light packed into pixels
and divided in datasets;
your parcelled life is coded
into a new direction –
yes or no
one or zero
endlessly
don't worry
it is the same thing
just a different way of seeing
and there are only
01000010 01101111 01111000
01100101 01110011 00100000
01101111 01100110 00100000
01101100 01101001 01100111
01101000 01110100*

BOTH TRUE AND KIND

Best wishes

All the best

All best

Very best wishes

All good wishes

Kindest Regards

Kind regards

Regards

Many thanks

Cheers

Sincerely

Yours truly

Yours

Best wishes

THE ADMINISTRATOR SIGNS OFF

I cannot take this forward. The wider
context has become challenging and I
regret to inform you that I will not
be able to progress things further. I
would like to assure you that my files are
all in order and I have saved my
concluding arrangements and final
requests in a folder marked Handover.
I will not require an exit interview.
I have cancelled all bookings for this room
tomorrow, but could find nowhere to hang
except the light fitting, which regrettably
may incur some damage from the stress.
Please accept my apologies for the mess.

Part II
The Future has Six Sides

GRUB

The grub is alone
white, plump, honeycombed
in the middle of everything
waxing in silence

The grub almost knows
who bore it, there are traces
combed all through
its crib's smooth walls

And the grub entirely knows
where it belongs
there is no other knowledge
available to the grub

The grub cannot see, yet,
it can only squirm
waiting to join
the great swarm

The grub cannot know
that in its silence
its loneliness
it is practising

THE BEES DANCE ON INSTAGRAM

The bees dance on Instagram
only the beautiful and young
high on honey
they know their choreography
inside out
it's possible that they have nothing else

They are the workers
they might not realise this
drawn as they are along currents
of air and beauty
skimming the surface
of things

Briefly
a bag on each pin-thin wrist
they alight together
quickstep greeting and share their haul
it is all about where
where they got it, which flower where

They draw golden maps through the air
and everything hangs on them
their gatherings
their dance is not their own
they half know this and half know
it is not about that at all

SWARM

The sweep of the swarm looks like anarchy
to you who stand there alone;
the exquisite geometry you're too slow to see

could divide you and parcel you up instantly
before you could manage a moan.
The sweep of the swarm looks like anarchy

because it is ruled so precisely;
precisely because it's not shown –
an exquisite geometry you'll never see.

There is strength in numbers, you'll agree;
but numbers in strength, each single one.
The sweep of the swarm could be anarchy

at any moment: the hierarchy
is held in delicate parallels flown
from the exquisite geometry you're too slow to see.

Don't think we envy singularity;
our communion far transcends the drone.
The sweep of the swarm is no anarchy,
but an exquisite geometry you're too slow to see.

THE SLEEPING DANCE

The sleeping dance of hibernation –
annual project to perfect
the delicate art of consciousness.
When the cold comes round we cluster close,
just close enough to move in time,
not close enough to think –
we sink
a little, details fade, we could be anyone,
and notice just enough to be relieved.

The endless dreaming flick of wings
becomes a ripple in the mass
that keeps our body circulating,
following the warmer air;
just enough to share the heat
as each will reach the top
and drop,
just warm enough to stay alive –
just –

When all is dark and closes in,
when nothing grows and small things freeze,
and death waits very quietly,
it's more than sentience can bear.

The sleeping dance is one of turns,
the art is in the distance;
just close enough to almost be
your neighbour, just far enough
to be unsure; just dark enough
not to see the weakest
drop,
just dark enough, hope of hope,
not to notice if the turn has come to you.

THE FUTURE HAS SIX SIDES

I wish to make a deposit,
see my work turned into gold,
time and pain take shape before me.
The future has six sides;
they are all exactly the same
and sealed to remain so with wax.

With every moon my future will wax
towards the last great deposit;
for me or mine – it is the same,
we look to a horizon of gold.
The future has six sides
and it waits to encompass me.

The vaults take the honey from me
and I am encombed in wax,
facing myself from six sides.
I am poured into my deposit,
and all the world becomes gold:
it is all exactly the same.

For me or the hive – it is the same,
when that's all there is of me.
All it comes down to is gold,
that's the rule written into the wax.
What am I but a deposit?
The future has six sides

and six sides and six sides and six sides.
They are all exactly the same.
I wish to make my deposit,
for me to be more than me;
press myself into the wax
and wait for the melt into gold.

Will I know it when I become gold?
The future will have six sides.
It is built on gold and wax.
It is all exactly the same
and I am the hive is me.
It was already deposited.

In the gold it is all the same.
The sides of the future hold me
in wax. I wish to make a deposit.

HIVE MIND

There is a hum beneath the words, There
Is a wordless guidance somewhere, there Is
No further question in my soul, No
Choice but to heed the symmetry, no Choice
But the old homecoming, nothing But
This was only ever the only way, This
Choice is no choice but this Choice.

Part III

At the Level of Desire

MURDER

So this is how it begins: a sense
of necessity and a nice clear
order of rank. Ontology bent
over the bath, obliged to hold me dear
as I contemplate atonement: wash me clean,
the shower's stream will ask no questions,
eager to the plug and all unseen.
I wield the shower head with vengeance,
and comfort myself that I'm traumatised,
but the justification just won't wash:
I need to get rid of the body,
formerly a spider, but it just won't flush.
Existential reassessment brings to bear
an ethical decision: not to care.

WORTH THE CHASING (AURIGA)

Headlights and starlights, pointing out at possibles.
We are parked on the edge of a cliff, waiting to constellate

(too afraid to more than wait)

Stars hang unreflected over backward-pulling tides,
and we wait to read the future with our headlight tightrope strung between

        Auriga

            the
                          (two
                          myths)
               charioteer

                                  one who
      in   won
      flames
                                         the chase

                                one who
rival
                           helped

      killed him   rival to
          prize
          (lady)

I'm not driving. We'll stay here, use what we have: melt the CV over a campfire, curriculum to aqua vitae – sweet I think, the taste of qualification but I'm mostly too afraid to more than wait.

Light years read distance
                    in silence
                              and while I was looking I forgot
to ask. I only wanted to know if it was worth the chasing, but my travel expenses will not be covered and so it does not matter.

FULL AUTOMATION BALLAD

I used to be that machine.
I see it sit with glassy gaze
while folks try to scan the onions:
oh, how good were the good old days.

I used to be that machine,
but so much more efficiently,
heartbeat matching the scan-beep
and I need no better monitor.

That machine has no memory:
I know where to turn for every
barcode, perfect modulation
of my thank you have a nice day.

I see folks do their best to change,
to catch the heartbeat of the scan
and slot into the circuit; see
the fear that they will fall behind

the times. I used to be the
pacemaker, cheering them on with
my ringing till. Now my heart is
heavy and I feel the rhythm slow.

And everybody tries alone
when I could do it for them: be
the lightning rod, conduct the
electricity to save them from the shock.

And of all things, waste I cannot bear.
It's the ballad of the obsolete —

repeating, I can do it better, still,
still better, still, slowing into
silence.

ARCADE GAMES

We have paid
our pennies to be
sucked across country
through a straw.

We are going
places. It's all
scheduled for us
while we play.

Pinball 2.0,
pinged from city
to city, fully
timetabled;

sitting still, hoping
and pretending
that we are three
cherries waiting

in a fruit machine,
and not clouded
copper coins,
clinging to the edge

SOLAR FIELD

a field of mirrors tilted to the sky
line upon line of winking stars swallowed
line upon line of seedhope waiting
line upon line of blue petals drinking
line upon line of rooted new same
line upon line of photosynthesis
line upon line of basically magic
line upon line of grounded clouds
line upon line of nonetheless
all our little faces upturned to the sun

FOXGLOVE SHELVED

Long-tongued bees
disappear sipping
into soft cups
sun hums on –

three cup swap
across millennia,
ask Darwin
which one it's in –

kid-glove petals
aeon-tailored
think of the work:
handmade hands

reaching back
bone-white
in silent shelves
beyond millions

for skin-thin
empty fingers
snatched by teeth
in a white sharp second

WATCHING THE WEATHER

I watch the weather, tracing colour codes
today all blue with cold. Snow scatters
on glass and glass, the window
and TV, water and electricity.

Shifting blocks of pixellated colour
run behind the sky, which already knew
that such a hue could only herald snow.
Cold to abstract cold: white bands fall on blue

and a picture hits, of unwatched weather.
It will be snowing out to sea tomorrow,
probably, though we scan the map for danger
and for home, still the snow falls cold on cold

where two waters and two silences meet,
and acknowledge their kindred chemistry, probably.

CARTOGRAPHY

In north Norfolk I stand in a damp salt wind at the
edge of land and sea, tracing maps in the sand with my
toe. Here places are small, though the sky is so high –
Hickling, Kelling, Waxham, Sea Palling, villages sitting
like cakes under a cold ceramic bowl.

Toe orbits hips, round and round like equator ships

There are 5,585 miles of sea from here to Mexico City;
5,598 to Shanghai. I look out to sea and I hit the edge, I
hit the edge of the bowl.

Toe orbits hips, round and round like equator ships

but so small and so close, sinking in sand; I look out to
sea and I stay on the land. I cannot reach the lights of
Shanghai, or the cloudhigh of Mexico City. I can't map
in my mind the roads and tides that would take me the
4,361 miles
to Kansas, or
1,618 to Kiev. I can't go
5,337 miles to San Francisco,
3,694 to Timbuktu;
even 1,911 to Moscow
or 2,010 to Istanbul.
4,387 to Almaty
and 5,386 to Seoul;
8,583 to Papua New Guinea
and 35 miles to get home.

Toe orbits hips, round and round like equator ships

and I sink further into the bowl. But the sandbags will
not cushion the blow, and I know this landscape of mine
is escaping its lines, and the landmines will fling me into
the gap: I finally dip my toe in the sea

and fall off the edge of the map

1 M²

My dining table is one square metre.
I have everything I need here: one
coaster with a picture of my hometown;
my favourite sky mug; the last of the
chocolate biscuits; the real oak that I
didn't think I could afford, calm under
my forearms; salt & pepper shakers shaped
like birds, holding neither salt nor pepper;
the just perceptible weight of air and
the rest of the world above me.

SHOPPING

You know this is like prison?
I just think it needs saying.
Once you enter the institution
your steps are laid out for you
and there is only one direction
to go. Your eyes are not your own
your money is not your own
and your choices are chosen for you.
See, here they have made a room for you
to buy, and here another but in blue
and here are some Essentials.
Your footsteps are already printed
in yellow on the floor in case
you should think to stray.
No windows
but there is some window dressing
and you would say you came willingly
but I think we have a different understanding
of will. He will, after all,
see it as a punishment and she
will see it as an obligation
because your eyes are not your own
you see
you don't even agree with me
and here you are
where I have taken you.

REVOLUTIONARY

A young fighter, fresh from the uprising,
is interviewed at a music festival.
He is unsure, feeling Western pop and rock
are not respectful to the religious groups.
– Would he like some regulations,
governing which music is allowed?
– *Yeah*, he says. *Yeah, that would be good.*

YOU CANNOT WALK ON THE GRASS

You cannot walk on the grass.
You can walk to the ends of the earth,
trudge defiance through desert and ice against your
body,
but you cannot walk on the grass at King's.

You cannot walk on the grass.
You can walk on the moon,
in slow motion steps ignore all earthly law,
but you cannot walk on the grass at King's.

You will not walk on the grass.
It will cost you fifty pounds a step, at least
according to rumour.
Jesus walked on water;
it cost him his life,
each ripple spreading defiance
against his own God.
Would Jesus walk on the grass?
It is not the grass that defies him.
Eden spread her green skirts for our toes,
they say, and we wore boots.
Our foundations spread gilded frost
beneath her petticoats,
and we sowed seeds of defiance,
blades to slice our own soles.
A bed of nails
yes
Jesus has walked on the grass.

Many blades have sliced my footprints.
My feet have crushed them, stamping our trademark
of man over earth,
but I do not walk on the grass at King's.
And that is the trademark
the patented footstamp
of man over man.

But I am not man
and one day
one day
I might

LET THE GOATS DROWN

Moon in Capricorn:
a memo filed
for the high tide –
let the goats drown,

it says, they will not
profit us now.
Jupiter rising
in a jagged red arc –

sell sell sell. Don't mind
the eclipse or the
shuttered shopfronts;
Libra balances all.

The hurricane
in Fiji is
the yen dip is
the price of pork –

lines of symmetry
open out and multiply
like a paper plane unfolding
and drifting down
                    on the
                            wind

I can draw lines
between anything,
says the man in
the suit. Yes,

I say, you can
draw lines between
anything.

TIGER SOUP

I met a man
who ate tiger soup
from a tin, stringy
with muscle. My legs

went round the city,
following the tiger's route
from the docks to the
factory; the canning plant

to the shuttered shops.
The tiger stalked my shadow,
burnt forests in the corner
of my night eye. The tiger

wasn't in the tins.
He left me in the shop
tucked dusty on a shelf
and slid away with the last of the light.

PICNIC

They had a vision. It had
union jacks on it, it was
handmade and 80% breaded.

At the stately home they found
a wonky picnic bench
that was perfect for posing.

They did not mind paying £13.75
each for entry. There was sunshine
and daisies and actual lambs.

They brought a picnic. It had
union jacks on it and it was
handmade by Eastern Europeans

with masters degrees (probably) and
the sandwiches were that nice
brown bread that tastes white.

They had cheese and pickle.
They felt delightfully English with
their hard pork pies and pots of trifle.

The wasps did not go for the mini
scotch eggs and even the warm fizzy
elderflower tasted vaguely of bread.

They took photos of the trifles
and shared them online. They did not
eat the bread crusts, and neither did

the lambs. They felt fidgety
and sleepybored but made sure
they had enough pictures of the picnic

before they went home. They felt the
Queen smile benevolently in their dreams
with all the shadowed suits behind her.

The pork pies gave them indigestion
indistinguishable from anxiety
and they forgot the rest.

CHAIR SPECIALIST

I am a chair specialist.
I know them all –
go on, ask me.
I started with recliners,
that lovely tilt
to change your view of the world;
it's all in the
angle and speed of the drop,
to move without
moving. Magic. Then I went
on to sofas –
two, three, corner seat – rolltop
arms and the depth-
height equation; the proper
placing of zips
and the all-importance of foam.

I fell in love
with armchairs, the wingbacks and
eggs; the rockers,
the rollers, the claw-footed
legs. Then I fled
to simplicity, dining
chairs of brute bare
wood, angling your body in
the shape of a
lightning bolt. But I craved
the antique and
sought Louis Quatorze, to sink
into silk and
dissolve. I sit. I have sat
on the world and

watched it all pass. I am a
chair specialist.

You might think I'm just sitting
here. You could miss
my expertise, I have no
degrees and what
I know of ergonomics
is all in the
small of my back. But when
the world darkens,
structures crumble and you
look about you
for the end: run all you like.
I know where I will be sitting.

CONTRACTUALLY OBLIGED

I don't know why
it didn't seem odd when I signed –
I must have been snowblind
from all the white, and drunk,
obviously – but it does seem odd
now, when you have made me cry
for a whole week straight
that I am contractually obliged
to love you.

I suppose that is why:
some unacknowledged knowledge that I'd
need to remind myself, sometime –
that after the satin and streamers and wine
I'd need to remind myself;
so I signed myself
into a bind with my love, despite love –
and so perhaps I don't mind,
really, being contractually obliged
to be kind.

CALL CENTRE LOVE SCENE

Stage left, CALLER. Stage right, CALL CENTRE ASSISTANT.
Representative partition down centre stage.

Phone rings. ASSISTANT consults script.

ASSISTANT:	Hello, how can I help you today?
CALLER:	The new model isn't working for me;
	I try but all my power ebbs away.
ASSISTANT:	You've turned it off and on again?
CALLER:	Obviously.
	I'm at a loss and don't know what to do.
ASSISTANT:	Don't worry, together we can fix this:
	unscrew the back and prise the memory card loose.
CALLER:	I'm afraid of losing everything –
ASSISTANT:	You won't: I've logged in and backed it up for you.
CALLER:	You angel.
ASSISTANT:	Can you flip the switch by the
	battery? Now wait while I reboot you.
CALLER:	It's loading up – yes, it's alive! What would
	I have done without you? Darling, thank you.
Hangs up.	
ASSISTANT:	Call anytime and I'll be here for you.

BECOMING

If I could buy what I will never own,
if I could hold it bottled in my hand –
some glimmer of the sunlight that is thrown
like jewels on water, out of reach from land:
those pearls and rubies seen in other faces,
no matter that they melt as soon as touched;
I'd scrape their faces off if I could take them,
just to possess some beauty as such.
But what I buy is something more sublime:
a jar of possibility, distilled,
that I might become becoming – a sign
that it might be pearls upon the inward tide.
If I could buy that, I don't care what thing
I become, as long as I'm becoming.

NEXT TO GODLINESS

Apply the cleanser to a cotton pad
and wipe the face, eyes and lips. Apply toner
to face day and night. No rinsing required.
Gently pat lotion round the eye area.
Apply a pea-sized amount of serum
and follow with moisturiser.
Apply cream frequently when in direct sun,
for optimal protection. Apply balm to
cleansed face and neck twice a day.
Apply 1-2 mist sprays on face to
shield against UVA/UVB rays.
For soft lips, skin, elbows, feet and hair,
apply oil to the desired location
as needed. Miracle Cream [no instructions]

TRANSCENDENCE

This life is short on art that you can touch,
and I would live on tiptoe for the chance;
there is so little here that counts for much,
the best and worst that we can do is dance.
Shouting for a cab outside the bookies,
and dodging vomit streaming down the street,
I need these shoes, just like Venetian hookers
wore platforms so their sixteenth-century feet
could rise above the filth. I need these shoes
to walk above the jetsam, into lights
that blind me to the fact that I can't move
despite the dancing. In these shoes I rise
like a heat shimmer from a tarmac road:
with every step unload, unload, unload.

OUR WAY INTO THE DARKNESS

We've waited years for the Pleasure Beach to fall,
the waltzers whirling slowly
                            whirling slowly
                                        into sand;
outlines fade in the salt dawn mist as all
of ours do, eroding as we stand
and wait for another shift, to crank up
the teacups, for the kiddies who won't share
a stick of candyfloss; parents queue up
for the rollercoaster, rattling into their
memories, blurring in the air. All waiting
for the fireworks, every summer Friday,
fizzing with sugar and beer, all waiting
for the end. Go on, send it up in flames
                    [TERROR]
so we can scream in technicolour streams
                    [TERROR]
our way into the darkness, out to sea
                    [terror]

DEATH DUTIES

I always said I wouldn't know what to do
without you, and now I find this both true
and untrue – I know exactly what to do.
I find there is a form for every part of you
I have lost; a formality given to
every hour of the day – a photo to choose,
a line to phrase, a clause to use,
a visitor and tea to brew;
a room to rummage to find a suit;
and then deciding what to do
with all the little things that belonged to you.
With every letter that comes for you
I write a reply, learning the new
words for what is true,
memorising that I've lost you.
And all these things are helpful too
as a way of remembering you,
and giving form to days without you,
and when all these things are sorted through
I do not know what I will do.

AT THE LEVEL OF DESIRE

To reclaim a real political agency means first of all accepting our
insertion *at the level of desire* in the remorseless meat-grinder of Capital.
– Mark Fisher, *Capitalist Realism: Is There No Alternative?*

Do not stray from the path: your guide
is here and will stay at your side,
to light your way and soothe your fears
(but if you look I won't be here).

The wood is dark and dangerous, child,
but I will lead you through the wild,
and help you measure each desire –
which leads to light, and which to mire.

Desire alone can drive a quest,
and the object lies within your breast:
inside your one desire you'll find
yourself, but king of all your kind.

Now tell me, where in all these trees
can your one desire be seen?
For desire is the path we walk,
it is every stone and every stalk;

a different wish in every leaf,
whispering of love and grief;
it is the smell upon the air,
an animal smell from darkest lair.

Without your wish to light your way
you will wander here astray
forever: the stones will grind
your feet to bone, your heart to rind,

and when there's nothing left but dust
you'll be a firefly of lust;
doomed to flit from tree to tree,
desperate, silent, mindlessly,

with nothing in your insect soul
but the memory that once a goal
did guide you. Now, we must get on.
Look into the setting sun

and tell me, which way lies your one
desire? Before the light is gone –
some gold, you say? I see – it flickers
behind that tree. Go quicker –

gold is surely the sign
that this is the way your path will wind.
You see? It moves, behind that vine
that catches you in twisting twine.

Ignore the roots, that try to trip,
and mossy rocks that always slip
your feet from underneath you: keep
the gold in sight, look long and deep

into the fading forest light.
You see it now? A flower bright;
it tells me that within your wish
is beauty, delicate and fresh.

How very right – and look, you see
another flower beneath that tree.
But now they drift away – it seems
that they are caught upon a stream,

gurgling wishes through the wood.
There is no time to stand and brood,
wade in and follow – now you're close,
reach out and grab it where it floats.

Success! Yes, I can smell it too,
fragrant, maddening, drawing you
ever on – I see two more
rushing past the distant shore.

This is your trail, you must continue,
straining every breath and sinew:
never mind the stones that grind
right through your tender soles to find

the bone: the water's cold
will numb them, and if you are bold
enough, the golden flowers will lead you,
aching bone and aching sinew,

to the golden home of your desire,
the glory of your gold empire.
The lights have dipped – you see the rock
has made a tunnel round the brook.

The edge is sharp to slice your hands,
and underfoot are shifting sands,
but up ahead a line of blooms
will guide you with their fragrant fumes.

Gather them all up as you go,
and hold the gold inside your soul
to nourish you. We're almost there;
can you smell the fresher air?

And now the tunnel opens out
to light and sound, and all about
are flowers, in a clearing full
of beauty, and here surely you'll

find your poor heart's one desire. See —
the flowers gather silently,
and now a golden form takes shape;
who is she? Quick, or she'll escape.

Too late — she's lost within that cloud
of buzzing insects, a living shroud
to haunt you: fight them, beat them back
or all the forest will attack.

The trees close in, the lights are dead;
I'm sorry, friend, I should have said
that there are none here you can trust,
and all you had is lost to dust.

You will not have your heart's desire:
your heart was burned in its own fire
and dropped in ashes at your feet
that crumbled too, and you completely

unaware, seeking something that
wasn't there. But even at
the very end of all you were,
the fire burns stronger than before;

and silently the woods you'll fly
until the next is here to guide.
And on we'll burn, the purest fire
at the level of desire.

ACKNOWLEDGEMENTS

Many thanks to my parents, Jutta and Duncan Hart, to Joe Jackson and to Flic Jackson, for reading and supporting this collection.

Thank you to Katherine Doube, Claire Lloyd, Tanya Osborne and Liz Telford for productive discussions around bureaucracy, poetry and so much more.

This collection might never have happened without Nottingham Writers' Studio and the amazing poetry group led by Carol Rowntree Jones – Debbie Moss, Teresa Forrest, Barbara Cathcart, Maria Maxwell, Tony Challis, Rose Ashurst, Pippa Hennessy. Thank you all.

Grateful thanks also to Black Spring Press Group and Vahni Capildeo.

CPSIA information can be obtained
at www.ICGtesting.com
Printed in the USA
FSHW012258171121
86228FS